MW01050424

# NURSERY
# RHYMES

A Random House PICTUREBACK®

# NURSERY

## Selected by Marie

Copyright © 1977 by Random House, Inc. All rights
reserved under International and Pan-American
Copyright Conventions. Published in the United
States by Random House, Inc., New York, and simul-
taneously in Canada by Random House of Canada
Limited, Toronto. Library of Congress Catalog Card
Number: 76-24168. ISBN: 0-394-83550-6.
Manufactured in the United States of America
7 8 9 0
C D E F G H I J

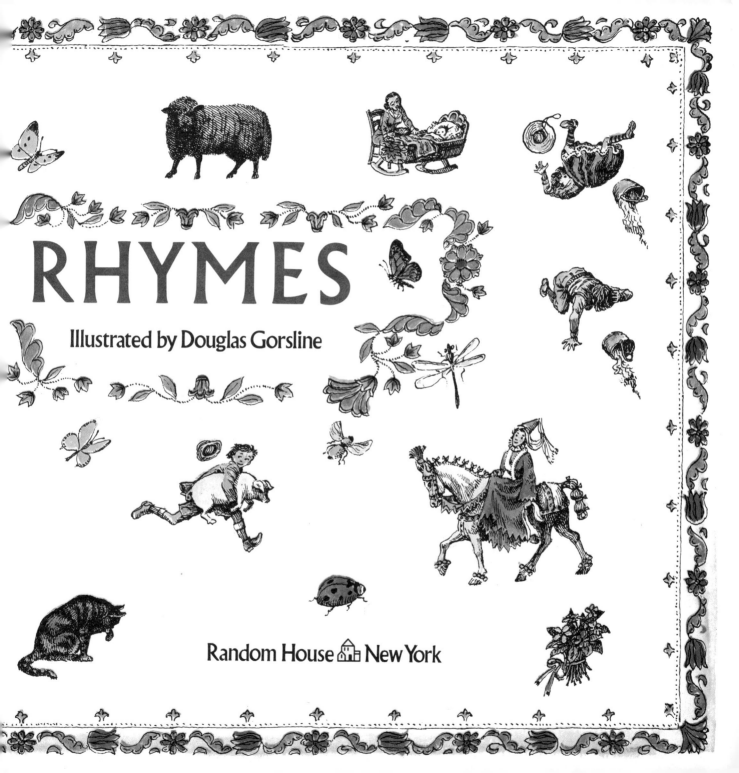

# RHYMES

Illustrated by Douglas Gorsline

Random House 🏠 New York

Little Boy Blue, come blow your horn,
The sheep's in the meadow, the cow's in the corn.
Where is the boy who looks after the sheep?
He's under the haystack, fast asleep.
Will you wake him? No, not I!
For if I do, he's sure to cry.

Little Bo-Peep
Has lost her sheep,
And doesn't know where to find them.
Leave them alone,
And they'll come home,
Wagging their tails behind them.

To market, to market, to buy a plum cake,
Home again, home again, market is late.
To market, to market, to buy a plum bun,
Home again, home again, market is done.

To market, to market, to buy a fat pig,
Home again, home again, jiggety jig.
To market, to market, to buy a fat hog,
Home again, home again, jiggety jog.

Ride a cock-horse to Banbury Cross,
To see a fine lady upon a white horse.
Rings on her fingers and bells on her toes,
She shall have music wherever she goes.

There was an old woman
Lived under a hill,
And if she's not gone
She lives there still.

A man of words and not of deeds
Is like a garden full of weeds.

He took him out of the stall
And put him on the wall,
And that's all.

There was an old man
And he had a calf,
And that's half.

Ding dong bell, Pussy's in the well.
Who put her in? Little Johnny Green.
Who pulled her out? Great Jack Stout.
What a naughty boy was that
To try to drown poor pussy cat,
Who never did any harm,
But killed the mice in his father's barn.

I like little pussy, her coat is so warm,
And if I don't hurt her, she'll do me no harm.
So I'll not pull her tail, nor drive her away,
But pussy and I very gently will play.

Elsie Marley is grown so fine,
She won't get up to feed the swine,
But lies in bed till eight or nine.
Lazy Elsie Marley.

Mary had a little lamb,
Its fleece was white as snow;
And everywhere that Mary went
The lamb was sure to go.

Baa, baa, black sheep,
Have you any wool?
Yes, sir, yes, sir,
Three bags full.
One for the master,
One for the dame,
And one for the little boy
Who lives down the lane.

Well, I never, did you ever
See a monkey dressed in leather?
Leather eyes, leather nose,
Leather breeches to his toes.

Round about, round about,
Gooseberry pie,
My father loves good ale
And so do I.

Up and down the city road,
In and out The Eagle,
That's the way the money goes,
Pop, goes the weasel.

Man's work lasts till set of sun.
Woman's work is never done.

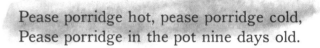

Pease porridge hot, pease porridge cold,
Pease porridge in the pot nine days old.

Magpie, magpie, chatter and flee,
Turn up your tail and good luck come to me.

A diller, a dollar,
A ten o'clock scholar,
What makes you come so soon?
You used to come at ten o'clock,
But now you come at noon.

There were two blackbirds sitting on a hill,
One named Jack, the other named Jill.
Fly away, Jack! Fly away, Jill!
Come again, Jack! Come again, Jill!

To fetch a pail of water;

Jack and Jill went up the hill,

Jack fell down and broke his crown,

And Jill came tumbling after.

London Bridge is falling down,
Falling down, falling down,
London Bridge is falling down,
My fair lady!

Build it up with iron and steel, iron and steel, iron and steel,
Build it up with iron and steel, my fair lady.

Iron and steel will bend and bow, bend and bow, bend and bow,
Iron and steel will bend and bow, my fair lady.

Build it up with gravel and stone, gravel and stone, gravel and stone,
Build it up with gravel and stone, my fair lady.

Gravel and stone will fall away, fall away, fall away,
Gravel and stone will fall away, my fair lady.

Oranges and lemons,
Say the bells of St. Clement's.
Halfpence and farthings,
Say the bells of St. Martin's.
When will you pay me?
Say the bells of Old Bailey.
When I grow rich,
Say the bells of Shoreditch.
When will that be?
Say the bells of Stepney.
I'm sure I don't know,
Says the great Bell of Bow.

What are little girls made of?
What are little girls made of?
Sugar and spice
And all things nice,
That's what little girls are made of.

What are little boys made of?
What are little boys made of?
Frogs and snails
And puppy dogs' tails,
That's what little boys are made of.

Bonny lass, bonny lass,
Will you be mine?
You shall neither wash dishes
Nor serve the wine;
But sit on a cushion
And sew a fine seam,
And feast upon strawberries,
Sugar, and cream.

Bobby Shaftoe's gone to sea,
Silver buckles on his knee;
He'll come back and marry me,
Bonny Bobby Shaftoe.

Bobby Shaftoe's strong and fair,
Waving back his yellow hair;
He's my love for evermore,
Bonny Bobby Shaftoe!

Diddle, diddle, dumpling, my son John,
Went to bed with his breeches on;
One shoe off, one shoe on,
Diddle, diddle, dumpling, my son John.

Go to bed, Tom.
Go to bed, Tom.
Tired or not,
Go to bed, Tom.

Bye baby bunting,
Father's gone a-hunting,
Mother's gone a-milking,
Sister's gone a-silking,
And brother's gone to buy a skin
To wrap baby bunting in.

Rock, rock, bubbly Jock,
Wake me up at ten o'clock.
Ten o'clock is far too soon,
Wake me up in the afternoon.

Little Miss Tucket
Sat on a bucket,
Eating some peaches and cream;
There came a grasshopper,
Who sat down beside her,
But she said, Go away or I'll scream.

Little Miss Muffet
Sat on a tuffet,
Eating her curds and whey;
Along came a spider,
Who sat down beside her
And frightened Miss Muffet away.

Mary, Mary, quite contrary,
How does your garden grow?
With silver bells and cockle shells,
And pretty maids all in a row.

How doth the busy bee
Improve each shining hour,
And gather honey all the day
From every opening flower!

Ladybug, ladybug,
Fly away home!

Your house is on fire,
Your children will burn!

Who killed Cock Robin?
I, said the sparrow,
With my bow and arrow.
I killed Cock Robin.

Who saw him die?
I, said the fly,
With my little eye.
I saw him die.

Who'll dig his grave?
I, said the owl,
With my pick and shovel
I'll dig his grave.

Who'll carry his coffin?
I, said the kite,
If it's not through the night,
I'll carry his coffin.

All the birds of the air
Fell a-sighing and a-sobbing,
When they heard the bell toll
For poor Cock Robin.

Tom, Tom, the piper's son,

Stole a pig and away he run.

The pig was eat and Tom was beat,

And Tom went howling down the street.

Oh, that I were where I would be,
Then I would be where I am not.
But where I am there must I be,
And where I would be I can not.

When I was a little he,
My mother took me on her knee;
Smiles and kisses gave me joy
And called me oft her darling boy.

Little Tommy Tucker
Sings for his supper.
What shall we give him?
White bread and butter.
How shall he cut it
Without any knife?
How shall he marry
Without any wife?

Wee Willie Winkie runs through the town,

Upstairs and downstairs in his nightgown;

Tapping at the window, crying through the lock,

Are the children all in bed, for now it's eight o'clock?

Hush-a-bye, baby, on the tree top,
When the wind blows the cradle will rock;
When the bough breaks the cradle will fall,
Down tumbles baby, cradle, and all.

Rock-a-bye, baby, your cradle is green,
Father's a nobleman, Mother's a queen;
And Betty's a lady, and wears a gold ring;
And Johnny's a drummer, and drums for the king.

Now I lay me down to sleep,
I pray the Lord thy child to keep.
Thy love guide me through the night,
And wake me with the morning light.

Sleep, baby, sleep,
Thy father guards the sheep;
Thy mother shakes the dreamland tree
And from it fall sweet dreams for thee,
Sleep, baby, sleep.

Twinkle, twinkle, little star,
How I wonder what you are!
Up above the world so high,
Like a diamond in the sky.
Twinkle, twinkle, little star,
How I wonder what you are!